THE BIG CONCERT

Written by
Kiki

Illustrated by
EMMANUEL FAVAS

Published by
Montbec Inc.

Publisher
MATT ARENY

Publication Advisor
JOSE AZEVEDO

Editorial Supervisor
ETHEL SALTZMAN

Artwork Supervisor
PIERRE RENAUD

ISBN 2-89227-226-2

THE BIG CONCERT

Chuck E. was now in Grade Two, and he spent part of his time at school singing in the choir and playing in the school, band. He enjoyed this very much. Music was a big part of his life. Mrs. Beaver often played the piano, and Mr. Beaver was a member of the Little Forest Fireman's Band. Chuck E. liked playing in the band, but he had never had to perform in front of anyone.

Band practice was at four o'clock every Tuesday and Thursday after school. Mrs. Groundhog was the band leader and she made certain that everyone practiced.

This was no problem for Chuck E. He enjoyed playing and looked forward to band practice. In fact, Chuck E. was always the first to arrive at band practice. He did this so that he could get in a few more minutes of practice time. Chuck E. was busy playing his recorder when Bobby walked into the band room.

"Hi, Chuck E!" Bobby shouted from across the room. "Haven't you had enough practice on that thing already?"

"Well, I guess so," Chuck E. replied, stopping his playing for a moment, "but I like to play all the time!"

"Not me," Bobby commented. "In fact, if we didn't have to take this silly subject, I wouldn't be here!"

"Well, Bobby, sometimes we have to do things we don't choose to," Chuck E. explained, "but that way we learn about all sorts of things, so that we can make up our minds whether we really like them or not."

11

"I guess you're right, Chuck E.," Bobby admitted. "But why do we have to play in front of the whole school and make fools of ourselves?"

"What?" Chuck E. exclaimed, looking very surprised. "Play in front of the whole school? Where did you hear that?" he asked nervously.

"Mrs. Groundhog told us after last practice," Bobby explained. "You had to leave early, remember?"

"Oh, yeah, I remember," Chuck E. said, staring blankly into space. "B-but I can't play in front of people, especially the whole school!"

"You have to, Chuck E.," Bobby tried to convince his friend. "You're the best in the band and Mrs. Groundhog wants you to do the solo!"

"Oh, no!" Chuck E. exclaimed anxiously. "I just can't! I would be too nervous to play!"

"But there's no one else who can do it!" Bobby pleaded. "You can't let the whole band down. And what about your parents?"

"My parents!" Chuck E. replied with surprise. "Will they be there too?"

"Sure!" Bobby answered. "The whole town's going to be there. This is the biggest concert of the year."

"Bobby, how am I going to do this?" Chuck E. asked, looking very upset. "I've never performed in front of people before. What if I freeze and can't play a note? I'll be so embarrassed!"

"Don't worry," Bobby said, trying to comfort Chuck E., "all of us will be a little nervous out there. You won't be the only one. If you start to get scared just look over at me and you'll see that you're not alone."

"O-Okay, but I'm going to need all the help I can get!" Chuck E. added.

"Well then, I'll get the whole band behind you." Bobby suggested. "Together we'll get you through it!"

"Thanks, Bobby, I certainly hope so," Chuck E. replied, without much conviction. Just then, the rest of the band members entered the room, followed by Mrs. Groundhog. They finished their practice for the day and, when it was time for everyone to head for home, Mrs. Groundhog came up to speak to Chuck E. in private.

"Chuck E.," Mrs. Groundhog told him, "you played beautifully today!"

"Why, thank you, Mrs. Groundhog," Chuck E. said gratefully.

"Chuck E., I wanted to mention the upcoming concert to you," Mrs. Groundhog continued. "I would like you to be our soloist. All the band members and I think that you are the best player we have."

"Well, I'm flattered, Mrs. Groundhog, but to tell you the truth, I don't know if I can do it" Chuck E. admitted ashamedly.

"I know how you feel," Mrs. Groundhog sympathized. "I was the same way when I was your age. My band teacher asked me to do the solo and I was so scared I thought I would never be able to. But my teacher convinced me that everyone is afraid the first time they have to perform in front of people. With the help of their friends and family, they learn to overcome it."

"Did you go on to play the solo in that concert, Mrs. Groundhog?" Chuck E. inquired.

"Yes, I sure did. And you know something? I didn't even make one mistake!" Mrs. Groundhog replied proudly. "And you can do it, too. Just remember you're not alone."

"W-Well, I'll try my best," Chuck E. finally agreed, still looking somewhat doubtful. "I just don't want to disappoint anyone if I make a mistake."

"You can only do your best, and that's all anyone can ask," Mrs. Groundhog reminded him. "We'll be proud of you, no matter what!"

"Thanks, Mrs. Groundhog," Chuck E. said, feeling a little bit better.

Chuck E. went home after school and told his parents all about the concert. They were thrilled to hear that Chuck E. had been chosen to play the solo.

"Son, we are so proud of you!" Mr. Beaver said with excitement. "We know you've been practicing hard and we hear how good you've become. We are going to be there right in the front row!"

"Thanks, Pop," Chuck E. replied
gratefully, "but could you and Mom and
Bonnie sit sort of in the middle. I'm
going to be nervous as it is, and if I see
you and Mom right in the front row,
I might be too nervous to play," he
explained.

"Okay, son, if that'll make you feel
better," Mr. Beaver agreed. "We know
how nerve-wracking these things can be,
and we wouldn't want you to be any more
uncomfortable."

"Thanks, Pop, I really appreciate it,"
Chuck E. said. "Now I'd better go and
practice if I'm going to play my best."

"That's my boy!" Mr. Beaver said with
pride, as Chuck E. went to his bedroom to
practice.

After a little while, Mr. Beaver realized that he wasn't hearing any sounds coming from Chuck E.'s bedroom. He wondered why Chuck E. wasn't practicing, so he went up to see. Chuck E.'s door was open, and he saw Chuck E. sitting quietly, staring out of the window into the dark night.

"Son, is there something wrong?" he asked with concern.

"Well, Pop, it's this concert," Chuck E. said, looking very troubled. "I don't know if I can go through with it! I mean, what happens if I can't play, once I stand up to do my solo?"

"Believe me, son, it won't happen,"
Mr. Beaver reassured him. "And you know
why? Because I'm going to give you
something that my father gave me when I
was your age, that helped me get over
being afraid!"

"What is it, Pop?" Chuck E. inquired
curiously.

"It's my 'Rock of Courage'!" Mr. Beaver
explained, pulling a small smooth stone
out of his pocket. "Ever since I was a
younster like you, whenever I needed the
strength to overcome fear, I would put my
hand in my pocket and hold onto this
stone. And every time I did that, I would
think of my father and the strength he
gave me. It always helped me feel
braver."

"Wow, Pop! Really? Do you think it could do the same for me?" Chuck E. wondered.

"I certainly do," Mr. Beaver assured Chuck E. "In fact, this stone must be stronger than ever, with both your grandpa's and my strength put together!"

"You're right!" Chuck E. exclaimed. "How can I fail with all of that behind me?"

"You won't fail" Mr. Beaver hugged Chuck E. tightly. "Now, how about getting to that recorder?" he suggested. "We don't want you to be rusty, do we?"

"Oh no, Pop!" Chuck E. said enthusiastically, as he ran over and picked up his instrument.

The next two weeks passed by very quickly. On the night of the concert, Chuck E. and the rest of the band arrived early to get in some extra practice so that they would be sharp. They took their places on stage, while everyone else made their way into the auditorium.

Mr. and Mrs. Beaver and Chuck E.'s sister Bonnie arrived and took their seats in the middle of the auditorium. Soon all of the other seats were full, too.

The curtains opened. Chuck E. looked out to see a large crowd of people staring at him. He felt nervous and scared at the thought of having to stand up in front of all those people. He put his hand inside his pocket and grabbed hold of his "Rock of Courage". As he felt the stone, he remembered what his father had told him. Within seconds he became less frightened. He realized that he wasn't alone and he had nothing at all to fear.

The concert began and was going well.
Soon it was time for Chuck E. to do his
solo. He stood up with pride and played
it perfectly. After he finished, the
audience applauded loudly, and Chuck E.
looked out to see if he could find his
parents in the crowd.

He finally noticed his father clapping
hard and smiling with joy. Chuck E.
smiled back and reached into his pocket
once again for his stone.

As he grasped it, he thought to himself, "Thanks, Pop! Thanks, Gramps! Thank you for all the strength you've given me."

Chuck E. would go on to use the "Rock of Courage" many times in his life. And one day he would pass it on to his son.

When you're feeling scared,

Just picture in your mind

Your family and friends who love you,

And you'll leave your fear behind.

Your friend,

Chuck E.